This book belongs to: _____

First Printing, 2016

Book 1 of the Habitat Series

Printed by CreateSpace.com

Illustrated by Merle "Brandon" Bandsma, Smiley Face Artwork

Dedicated to my gecko living upstairs, who sparked my imagination and brought this story to life.

One dawn, Mama Gecko was tucking Little Gecko into bed after he had been playing outside all night.

"Mama, guess what?" Little Gecko said.

Mama Gecko chuckled, "What, Little Gecko?"

"I want to be a coyote," Little Gecko said, as he gazed from the branches of his home at the soon to be rising sun.

"And why is that Little Gecko?" Mama asked, curiously.

"Because Big Coyote sings to the moon with his beautiful voice, and I'd love to be able to sing," Little Gecko stated dreamily.

"But then you would not be able to chirp to me, and I love to hear your own chirping song," Mama said.

"Well, I guess you are right, Mama." Gecko said with a sigh. "I do like to chirp to you."

"Goodnight, Little Coyote"

"Goodnight, Mama."

The next dawn, Little Gecko scampered into bed and excitedly exclaimed, "Mama, I want to be an owl."

"Oh really? And what is so great about being an owl?" Mama replied, sitting on Little Gecko's bed.

"Well, Soaring Owl can fly high in the sky above the trees."

"Yes, Little Gecko, but you like to climb high in the trees. Your cute, little, sticky toes help you to hang onto things, even upside-down. Don't you love to hang upside-down?"

"Yes, Mama. Yes, I do." Little Gecko said, as he was currently hanging upside-down.

"Goodnight, Little Owl," Mama said, as she tucked him in and gave him a hug.

"Goodnight, Mama," Little Gecko replied almost asleep already.

As the sun rose the following day, Little Gecko galloped into his room and tried hopping onto his bed. Mama Gecko, who was waiting for him, chuckled with delight.

"Are we a jackrabbit today, Little Gecko?"

"Oh no, Mama. I'm a kangaroo rat. I saw Jumping Kangaroo Rat eating seeds and grass. It looked delicious." Little Gecko said, as he was licking his lips.

"I am sure Jumping Kangaroo Rat's grasses and seeds looked tasty, but I think you would prefer your insects, Little Gecko." Mama said, patting Little Gecko's head.

"Maybe you are right, Mama. They are good."

"Goodnight, Little Kangaroo Rat."

"Goodnight, Mama."

This dawn, Little Gecko came racing into his room and jumped onto his bed.

"And what are we today, Little Gecko?" Mama Gecko asked.

"I want to be a roadrunner. Speedy Roadrunner can play during the day. Wouldn't that be fun?" Gecko said as he watched the sun rise over the hills.

"Yes, but Speedy Roadrunner gets hot during the day and wants shade. Wouldn't you rather sleep during the day and play beneath the moon and stars you love so much?"

"I never thought about that Mama," pondered Little Gecko.

"Goodnight, Little Roadrunner."

"Goodnight, Mama."

The following dawn, Little Gecko tried to slither his way to his bed.

"So, let me guess, Little Gecko. You want to be a snake."

"I don't want to be just any snake, Mama. I want to be a rattlesnake," Little Gecko replied, trying to find a way to slither onto his bed.

"And why is that?"

"Because Sly Snake is so brightly colored and shakes his tail to keep predators away." Little Gecko tried wiggling his tail, but no sound came.

"That is true, Little Gecko; they do have pretty colors. You have a special talent they don't have. You can change colors to blend in with the land around you. Isn't that fun?" Mama asked as she picked Little Gecko up and put him on the bed.

"I guess you are right, Mama."

"Well, I think you make a better gecko anyway."

"Thanks, Mama."

"Goodnight, Little Rattlesnake."

"Goodnight, Mama."

Little Gecko came inside from playing the next night and laid down into his bed.

"And who are you today, Little Gecko?"

"Oh Mama, I'm a gecko. I love being just the way that I am."

"I agree, Little Gecko. I love you just the way that you are as well."

"Goodnight, Little Gecko." Mama said as she kissed his forehead.

"Goodnight, Mama."

A note from the authors:

We hope you like our story about the Little Gecko. He has many friends in other habitats that we are working on bringing to life as well. Look for them in the future.

Made in the USA
San Bernardino, CA
03 December 2016